The Tale of the GOLDEN BILLIKEN

Along with a few other Nome, Alaska Tales.

BY

LEON BOARDWAY

Printed and bound in the United States of America
First printing • ISBN # 978-1-954463-21-9

Along with a few other Nome, Alaska Tales.

EMAIL: EECHILLYLEE@GMAIL.COM

BY

LEON BOARDWAY

SCOTT PUBLISHING COMPANY
www.scottpublishingcompany.com
P.O. Box 9707 • Kalispell, MT 59904
Toll Free: 1-800-628-0212
Fax: 1-406-756-0098

DEDICATION

I dedicate my book to my Children and to all visitors over the years that have visited Nome and to those that have yet to visit Nome.

CONTENTS

PROFILE OF A FINE CITY

The yell of "Gold" echoed over the land. Thousands made their way across the tundra and the sea to a place rich in Gold. Right after the Three Swedes first discovered Gold, tents sprang up along the beaches, forming a city called Nome. The tents turned into buildings and Time turned into Progress with businesses of all types. Mercantiles, restaurants, stables, hotels and saloons nestled against each other forming streets and avenues.

Each ship that came to Nome brought more people, supplies and lumber, thereby enlarging the demand for new buildings and houses. Although many lived on their mining claim or out in one of the mining camps, they would still come in for a couple of days for supplies and maybe a night on the town. The enjoyment they must have had watching the "Dance Hall Girls" kicking their legs to the beat of a fast-fingered piano player, playing loudly over the sounds of the roulette wheel, dice table or just the howls of laughter on this special night.

Many departed Nome after fires and storms claimed their toll but many stayed, building and rebuilding a place to call home.

NOME, ALASKA

'There's No Place Like Nome'

The Tale of the GOLDEN BILLIKEN

Now, let's begin at the beginning. Some call him Goldilocks. Some called him a crook. But to his pals down at the old Board of Trade Saloon where he worked as a weigher of gold dust, he was called the Yellow Kid. He would weigh out your gold, exchanging it for cash. But he had one little trick up his sleeve. He would grease down his hair with polar bear grease. You would hand him your poke. He would pour a pile of gold on the table, then with his fingers he would move the gold around at the same time pushing the gold up into his fingernails, then he would pour the gold onto the scales to weigh it. He would hand you the cash then run both of his hands through his hair. By the end of the night his hair would be sparkling with all the gold struck in the grease.

He would go home, pull out the basin and wash all that gold right out of his hair! This went on night after night, from the beginning of the Rush till the year of the big fire, when practically the whole city of Nome burnt to the ground. The tale of the golden Billiken rises from those ashes.

One night the Yellow Kid was out on the town with his buddy "Hello Central." The kid mentioned that he had all this gold and was afraid to haul it out where a curious person might ask where he had gotten it from. At about this time, an old Eskimo carver, maybe even the famous Andrew Kunayak himself, came up and wanted to sell an ivory Billiken. When the kid first saw that Billiken, he automatically began to hatch a plan to sneak out the gold. He would make a mold in the shape of a Billiken, then fill it up with melted gold.

Everything seemed all right until the "Irish Cowboy" showed up in town one night and took "La Rene" the hatcheck girl over at the Northern Saloon by the arm and out the door, stepping over "Sleepy Pete" and bumping into old "Rubber Legs." They were laughing and having a good old time as they made their way down the wooden sidewalk to the Board of Trade Saloon. That is the one thing you really didn't want to do, because La Rene was the Yellow Kid's gal. At least that is what he thought.

Pig Eye John the bartender at the Northern must have had sent word to the Kid because he was some kind of mad when they appeared in the doorway of the Board of Trade. The Yellow Kid was drinking a bottle of whiskey with one hand and twirling his six-shooter in the other. He was so mad that he almost shot himself in the mouth when he got his hands mixed up and took a drink from his six-shooter. Needless to say, he started to point that six-shooter at the Irish Cowboy when up walked Wyatt Earp, who was a friend of them both. Wyatt said, "Hey boys, what's up? Are you a-drinking or a-fighting?"

"I'm a-drinking," said the Irish Cowboy. "And I'm a-fighting," said the Yellow Kid. "Well, I'm a-leaving," said Wyatt as he walked across the street towards the Dexter Saloon. That's the one thing Wyatt didn't need to get himself involved in. He always had trouble keeping his Tombstone reputation in Tombstone. As soon as Wyatt crossed the street, the Irish Cowboy and the Yellow Kid started going at it. The fists were flying. Then a shot rang out. The bullet just missed the Irish Cowboy by inches, ricocheting off the big clock in front of Veronica's jewelry store, flying over to Miss Dunaway's boarding house and landing right in the only fur-lined honey bucket in town.

It was kind of funny seeing Miss Dunaway come rushing out the door with her broom raised over her head ready to sweep the Kid right off his feet. The Marshall came running out of the Polar Cub Café where he was just finishing a big spaghetti dinner. With both of his guns drawn and spaghetti dangling from his beard he was ready to shoot anything that moved. He had one pistol aimed right at the Kid and the other aimed right at the Cowboy. Wyatt came running back from across the street hoping to calm things down, but the Marshall said, "Wyatt, that's fur enough. Don't make another move." Old Wyatt wasn't used to being treated that way and told the Marshall where he could go, which was a much warmer place than Nome. That seemed to make the Marshall madder than the shooting, and after a little scuffle he arrested Wyatt for interfering with a Peace Officer. You could hear Wyatt saying OK, OK, as the Marshall led him away towards the jail down past the Nome Ice House and Delivery Stable right before you get to St. Joe's Church. Big Dave the Driller shouted out, "Somebody better go and find Josephine Earp down in one of those gambling joints to come and bail Wyatt out."

Stagger Lee shouted back, "I'll go fetch her, she's probably down at the Bering Sea Saloon playing Faro with Sabo."

Now, let's get back to the Yellow Kid. Knowing that his days were numbered and fearing that La Rene might talk about the gold, he decided to start setting his plan in motion and slipped out of the crowd during all the commotion. He went up to his room at the Golden Gate Hotel, one of the largest and grandest hotels in Nome. Once in his room, he pulled out from beneath the bed eight 20-pound sacks of gold. He lit the burner under the melting pot that he bought at Nome Builders Supply, the only store in town that carried everything a person would need in the Far North. Slowly but gently, he began pouring the gold into the pot, occasionally stirring it like he was mixing frosting for a wedding cake. The hotter the pot grew, the quicker the gold melted. This wasn't easy work by no means. He had to pour, stir and at the same time keep his ears open for the sounds of anyone walking up the stairs.

From the closet he pulled out the mold for the Billiken. A few days earlier he had Carl Iyakitan, an Eskimo ivory carver from the village of Gambell on St. Lawrence Island, carve out a mold from a huge tree stump that had washed up on shore down by Fort Davis on a little stretch of beach they call Poor Man's Paradise. When Carl finished carving the mold, the Yellow Kid paid him off and Carl paddled his kayak back home to Gambell across the Bering Sea.

Filling the mold with the melted gold was going as planned. Now all the Kid had to do was wait for the gold to cool down and harden. But the Yellow Kid forgot one thing. How was he going to carry the Billiken out of his room, and where was he going to take it? He then remembered his pal Charley digging in the basement, leveling the ground to put in a new floor next summer. He would carry the Billiken to the basement and bury it, and when summer approached, he would simply dig it up and carry it out like a big bag of laundry to the boat. But first, how was he going to carry it down to the basement? Then he thought he would kill two birds with one stone so to speak. He would make friends with the Irish Cowboy, then take him into his confidence by offering him a share of the gold. The Kid figured he would have him help carry the Billiken down to the basement. First bury the Billiken, then the Kid would turn around and bury the Irish Cowboy alongside of it. He figured that it would take the two of them to carry it, but only one of them to bury it.

Now that was a plan.

So, the Yellow Kid set out to find the Irish Cowboy while the melted gold slowly cooled into a work of art. The first place the Yellow Kid went into was Tex Rickard's Northern Saloon. Tex was sitting at a card table in the corner. "Hey Tex, you seen the Irish Cowboy anywhere around?" the Kid asked. "Nope," said Tex as he raised the pot $5000. Old Billy Smith said, "I seed him down by the Anchor Tavern a little while ago, hanging onto Little Annie." With that he threw in $10,000 dollars' worth of chips and said, "I'll see your 5 and raise you 5 more."

Anyway, the Yellow Kid walked over to the Anchor Tavern and there bellied up to the bar was the Irish Cowboy with his arms around Little Annie. The Kid approached them and calmly and sincerely stuck out his hand. Then he said, "Hey Cowboy, I'm truly sorry about what happened earlier. Please accept my humble apologies and allow me to buy you a drink." The Irishman didn't quite understand what the Kid said, but he knew what "buy me a drink" meant. So, he shook his hand and replied, "I'll take a double. One for me and one for my beautiful Little Annie." Only Woody the Bartender at the Anchor noticed the sinister look that flashed in the Yellow Kid's eyes as he poured the first of the many rounds that would follow into the early hours of the morning. Matter of fact, Woody had to send Frankie the Gofer down the street to the Anchor Liquor Store to replenish his stock of Alaskan Amber.

Like I was saying, the party was on. Little Annie caught the smile of Mike the Miner, who had just come in from his claim behind and below Anvil Mountain. The Kid and the Cowboy decided to mosey on down to the Breakers Bar for a couple, then down to the Polar Bar for a couple, then up to the Board of Trade Saloon for a couple more. The B.O.T was a-hoppin' and the champagne corks were a-poppin.' Jim West the owner was weighing the gold dust and Jimmy his son was pouring the booze along with Amy, Veronica and Betty D'Boop, the prettiest bartenders in Nome, Alaska. And if you were to look just right, you could see Jim West's hair beginning to sparkle under the dim lights.

Now I mentioned that the prettiest bartenders were down at the B.O.T. but the prettiest gal in the Far North was called Buckaroo Gail. Now she was the toast of the town with a beautiful smile that melted many a miner's hearts in this frozen land. The Irish Cowboy took one look and fell head over heels for her. When he picked himself up off the floor he said, "If beauty was but a piece of pie, you would be a la mode." She told him that he better take it easy because she was Eskimo and Irish from Little Diomede Island. Then she told him in words he could understand. If it was a woman he wanted, he should go to the whorehouse down the street and upstairs from the Pioneer Coffee Company, where the women were fresh in the evening and the coffee was fresh in the morning.

The piano player was playing loudly over all the noise in the saloon when the Yellow Kid grabbed the Irish Cowboy by the arm and said to him, "Before you take off anywhere, I need your help to carry something from my room over at the Golden Gate. We just need to take something down to the basement; it won't take long. So be a good man and I'll give you a shot. Hell, I might make that a double."

"Alright!" said the Cowboy, "Let's go." Now it was a late September evening and the wind was a-howlin' like wolves chasing down a herd of caribou. Across the street they went. When they got to the Golden Gate Hotel, they decided to have one drink in the bar. Old Stud Duck was tending the bar that night when the Kid shouted, "Hey Bartender, give us a drink." Old Stud Duck replied in his slow Southern drawl, "Hold on to your malamutes boys, I'll be there in a minute." While the two waited in came the Marshall. He noticed them leaning against the bar. "Well, it looks like you two have made up or you're up to no good," he said. Little did he know that he was half right.

Old Stud Duck came up and said, "Whata ya'll having there fellers?" The Kid replied, "I'll have a triple. One for me, one for him and one for the Marshall." They all gulped their drinks down and licked the remnants off their lips at the same time saying, "Ahhhh!" as though it was a big bite of apple pie. The Yellow Kid excused himself and snuck back upstairs to check on his masterpiece, finding that it was still too hot to handle. He needed to figure out a way to stall for more time. So, he walked out the door and as he was thinking he started down the stairs. He missed the top step and without any grace he tumbled all the way down to the bottom. Then the thought struck him like a Dempsey punch. "Yeah," he thought, "we'll do the Nome Shuffle." Now the Nome Shuffle for those of you who don't know, consists of starting on one end of the street and having a drink or two in every bar until you reach the other end of the street. Some call it Uptown going Downtown. Or if you started on the other end, it was Downtown going Uptown. Either way, to most that was pretty much a night on the town.

At about this time the Ice Cream Lady came running over to give the Kid a helping hand. Pulling him up she said, "Wow, that was a pretty good fall, are you all right?" The Kid replied, "Reminded me of a Rocky Road." They both got a good chuckle out of that. Then the Kid staggered into the bar. He shouted, "Come on Cowboy, we're going to do the Shuffle."

"All right!" Cheered the Irish Cowboy. "Where do you want to start?" he added. The Kid said as he motioned with his hand, "Let's start over at the Polaris and make our way back down to the BOT." But in the back of his mind he knew that they couldn't make it all the way to the Board of Trade Saloon. They could probably make it halfway, which would pretty much bring them back to the Golden Gate Hotel. So, off they went into the cold night. The wind really began to blow while they were inside, making the Kid and the Cowboy lean into it as they walked. Their unbuttoned coats were flapping in the wind making them both look like a couple of drunk ostriches looking for a hole to stick their heads in. Out of breath but not out of money, they finally made it to the Polaris Bar.

Once inside they noticed Old Norm sitting there. "Hey Norm. How the hell you been?" they both asked. Norm replied, "Not bad, you boys been staying out of trouble?" The kid said, "I'll take the Fifth." And the Irish Cowboy said, "I'll take the Fifth too. As a matter of fact, I'll take two fifths. A fifth of R&R and a fifth of Jameson." Their next stop was at the Bering Sea Saloon where they ran into Stagger Lee trying to pry Josephine away from the Faro Table, with her saying, "Tell Wyatt I'll be down to bail him out as soon as this table cools off. No sooner, no later…Hey Colo, set us up a round. I'll take a quadruple. One for me, one for Stagger, one for the Cowboy and one for Yellow Kid." Well, doing the shuffle you really don't stay in one place too long. So, they downed their drinks and with their hat in their hand each gave Josephine a little peck on the cheek. The Kid said, "I'll see you later" and the Cowboy whispered, "I'll see you sooner!" Then out the door they went, making a b-line right to the Nome Grocery & Liquor Store.

"Hey Joan, we be needing two cigars and a pint of Jack for a chaser."

Now Joan had the biggest kick watching the two of them trying to light their cigars in the wind that seemed to be blowing even harder. Giving up, they threw down their unlit cigars and headed for the Anchor Tavern. What a sight, arm in arm. One was walking forward and the other one was walking backwards. When they got to the door of the Anchor they couldn't remember if they were going in or coming out. Needless to say, they just kept on walking but not far, maybe five steps when they came upon the Breakers Bar. Earlier that night the Champagne Kid bought all the girls in the bar a bottle of the very best champagne. He struck it rich and now he wanted everyone to feel rich like him. Even if it was just for the night and just for the girls. One time he hit a big strike, came into town and bought every bottle of champagne in town so Little Annie could take a bath in it. It took her four days to get out of the bathtub, and when she did, she looked like a raisin. Some say that they just rebottled it and sold it as pink shampoo.

The Yellow Kid stood by the window looking over at the Golden Gate Hotel across the street. "Come on Cowboy, let's go over to my room so you can help me carry that thing down to the basement." So out the door they waltzed. And I mean waltzed. Three steps forward, one step backwards. Then when they got to the door, side step, side step. Anyhow, they got outside where they ran into Miss Mamie. Now Miss Mamie Malony ran the Roadhouse down at Safety about thirty miles east of Nome. She also ran the ferry that got you across the river. So, you better be nice or you won't get back across. But that's not why everyone loved her. It was because she was always so nice and friendly to everyone. The Kid and the Cowboy stepped to the side giving a cockeyed bow while saying, "Good evening Madam, how do you do?" Mamie knew just what type of characters they were and simply smiled then said, "You boys better not be misbehaving, the water's rising."

"No, we ain't," they said as they were trying to recover from their bows. Now, crossing over to the hotel and after a few of the normal hurdles, like stairs, doors and any obstacles in their path, they finally made it to the room. There sitting on the burner in the pot was the golden Billiken, shining as though it had every ounce of gold ever taken out of Nome melted in it. The Cowboy stopped dead in his tracks as soon as he walked in. The only light was from the oil lamp, which made the Billiken look much larger than it really was. He didn't know if he was supposed to shake its hand or offer the dang thing a drink.

"What the tarnation is that thing?" the Cowboy asked quizzically. "Oh, oh that's what I need your help for. You see if you rub its tummy and bury it, it will bring you good luck. That is why we need to take it to the basement and bury it. And since we are buddies, I wanted to share the good fortune with you. Now come on, you grab the bottom and I'll grab the top, then place it on the bed. OK, on the count of three, a one, a two, a three," sounding like Louie Green, the band leader down at the Polar Bar playing Wooly Bully with Art the Ambassador.

Anyway, up came the Billiken from the pot. The two of them carried it to the bed after a couple minutes of weaving and bouncing off the walls. Once placing the golden Billiken on the bed, they wrapped it with the red bedspread as it wobbled on the old spring mattress, making it hard to handle. But the Kid and the Irish Cowboy also wobbled and once they all got in unison, they didn't have a problem.

At about this time, the Irish Cowboy started to think about what was going on. So, without the Kid knowing, he took the letter opener from the table and scratched the golden Billiken's big toe. Sure enough, this has to be solid gold he thought. "Maybe what I'll do is bury the Kid with it. Yes…now by-golllly that's a plan."

A one a two and a three. The two of them picked up the golden Billiken and headed as quietly as they could to the basement. I would describe the trip down, but let's just say that the Billiken's toes weren't the only ones that got scratched or mashed that night. We won't even mention the hole they made in the wall or the words that they were painfully whispering under their breaths as they made their decent. And they weren't just saying, "Ouch, ouch!" Finally, they made it to the basement with the Cowboy stumbling off the last step, picking himself up saying, "Wow, what a trip."

They set the golden Billiken down and started digging a hole in which to place their golden treasure in. Once done, they both slowly pulled out their revolvers as they turned, pointing and aiming at arm's length at each other's head. What they didn't know was that while they were digging, the whole town above them was on fire. Some say it was a moonshiner still that blew up, others say something in a room at the hotel blew up. But anyway, the whole town was now engulfed in flames.

The fire was so big and bad that Fire Chief Lewis had to get Big Bill Troffer the blaster to dynamite some of the buildings to try and stop the walls of flames moving in all directions. When he got to the hotel, Fire Chief Lewis said, "OK Trof, you better throw about five sticks of dyno in here."

The Kid and the Cowboy didn't have any clue as to what happened. But as they were standing there with their guns drawn and triggers being pulled back, all of a sudden there was a big Ka-Boom! And you should have seen the looks on their faces as they both flew up and out about a hundred fifty feet apart, tumbling like acrobats doing back flips with their arms a-flappin' and landing in the middle of the street on fire.

Seeing this, the bucket brigade rushed over and poured about ten buckets of water on each of them. Laying there in a daze they tried to remember exactly what had happened. They both had the same strange thought. They were digging a hole to bury something, something big and gold, in a basement. Was it under one of the saloons or one of the hotels? Try as they might, they just couldn't remember exactly what they were burying before being catapulted into the smoke-filled morning air.

There weren't any city maps, and after the fire no one knew where any of the buildings once stood nor where the golden Billiken was buried. Some said they thought they heard the Irish Cowboy mumbling as they were pouring buckets of water on him, "Hey Thanks for the chaser. We buried a golden Billiken. Lots of stairs." Gurgling he said, "There's No Place like Nome."

The Yellow Kid eventually regained his consciousness and having the same mental block as the Irish Cowboy, wandered around Nome for a while, and after leaving it is said that he became the manager for Jack Dempsey, the most famous boxer that ever was. Tex Rickard, the owner of the Northern Saloon in Nome and Madison Square Garden in New York, became a famous boxing promoter. He and Jack became the best of friends with Tex promoting most of his fights. Tex himself never did get along with the Yellow Kid.

I would like to say that this tale was true but like all tales you got to chase them. All I can say is that every person in this tale has been in Nome at one time or another. It never ends…

A NIGHT OF POKER

It all started one night when Little Annie, Good Time Charley, and Big Jack "Loud" McCloud were down at the Board of Trade Saloon having a couple of drinks. McCloud heard through the grapevine that a big poker game was going on at Tex Rickard's Northern Saloon. Now a big poker game would be the place to go, but the B.O.T. was the place to be. McCloud knew all too well that a big poker game would last for days, and if it just started everyone would be fresh, so he decided to wait for a few hours for them to get tired, drunk or broke. Another fact was that McCloud and Tex had a falling out earlier that winter. They were good friends but not at the moment. There was talk that McCloud owed Tex some money from a trip to Hot Springs, Arkansas they took together. They went down there to bet on some big horse race and when they came back they were mad at each other, but whatever happened is their story... what's going to happen is another story.

You see it was a big night. The town was celebrating the finish of a big dog race up over the Iditarod Trail. The party was on and so were the taps. Good Time Charley was thinking to himself, while Annie was trying to figure out some way to get a stake for that there poker game. She knew she wasn't a great poker player, but she was the best Snerts player on the Seward Peninsula. Now all it took was money. Annie was thinking, "It ain't no penny ante, Annie," which means at least a couple pokes of gold dust just to get in the game. Then she started thinking, "Where is that Charley?!" Annie never worried about Good Time Charley. It was Plain Old Charley she always worried about. The B.O.T. was so crowded and Annie, not being very tall, couldn't see over everyone, so she stood up on the bar to see if Charley was on the other end. She wasn't about to lose Charley in the saloon.

Now, while Annie was trying to get her balance, she looked like she was doing some kind of new dance with her arms waving all around. The crowd started cheering and throwing gold nuggets at her feet. Once Annie regained her balance, the show was over. "Hey J.D. What's all these nuggets doing here?" Little Annie asked J.D. the bartender. "It's for the show you put on," he replied. Confused, Annie asked, "What show?"

"I don't know. I was down at the other end loaning Charley some gold so you could get into that poker game," J.D. said as he walked away shaking his head. "Yep, that's my Charley," Annie thought. She started picking up those nuggets and putting them in her Crown Royal bag full of bingo markers that she always carried around with her. You could never tell when a big bingo game might pop up. Annie turned around and Charley was standing there with a poke of gold hanging from his outstretched hand. Charley said, "Annie, here's a poke for that poker game." Then Annie said, "I ain't playing if you ain't playing... Whatta ya say we split it?"

"Yep, that's my Annie!" Charley said to himself. Annie couldn't tell him about the gold nuggets in her bag because she couldn't really figure out the whole thing herself, but when she did… she'd tell him. Or… not. But now was not the time. Little Annie only had two times: good times and bad times. And for sure, Annie wouldn't let the bad times get in the way of the good times. She always said… "It's just a waste of time."

Annie grabbed Charley by the arm and motioned him towards the door and yelled, "Hike!" And just like the leader of a dog team heading home, he maneuvered Annie though the crowd and safely out the door. Once outside, they bumped into their old pal Pushatruck leaving the poker game over at the Northern Saloon. Good Time Charley said, "Do any good?" Pushatruck said, "All I could do was watch my money grow scarce," as he was making his way though the crowded sidewalk. "Come on Charley," Annie said. "We're gonna make our fortune tonight!"

Charley was still in the lead, and with Annie holding on tight they started their adventure into the night. Now walking on those wooden sidewalks was quite a deal. You had no orderly flow and everyone was polite so there was a lot of head nodding, hand shaking and Annie got her share of "How do you do, Madame?"s. It took a good 15 minutes of hobnobbing before they finally made it to the Northern Saloon, which was only two doors down. There it stood, a fine big building.

About that time, "Loud" McCloud as they called him showed up. He pushed Annie and Charley off to the side and grabbed the only empty seat at the table. Loud McCloud pulled out all the gold he had to his name, then threw it on the green cloth table and said, "Here Tex, weigh this gold dust and give me some chips." Tex called his gold weigher over and told him, "Weigh this stuff and chip him." Loud McCloud yelled over to the weigher and said, "Chip me, not jip me." Tex took offense to that and told McCloud to cool it. Loud McCloud didn't say anything, he just kinda grunted and ordered a triple shot of whiskey. The bartender said, "Hey McCloud, you want a chaser?" and Loud McCloud said, "No, I'll chase her later. I got a poker game to play. On second thought, you better give me a bucket of beer with that."

Now back to the game. Tex was at the card table along with Alapa Amy, who had the night off from the B.O.T. Big Al was there chewing on a five dollar cigar. He said it lasts longer if you don't light it. Sitting next to him with a big stack of chips was Buckaroo Gail, who came over the

Iditarod Trail. Glue Pot Tony looked like the big winner so far, with stacks of hundred dollar chips in front of him. Billy Smith was there but a beauty caught his eye, so he cashed in and went out. "Now there's an opening," Annie said, as she grabbed the chair and sat down before anyone else did. She didn't want to wait days for another opening. Like they say: someone is going home a winner, it just might take them a week to get there.

Anyhow, Annie threw her bingo bag down on the table and said, "Here you go boys. Weigh this." The weigher grabbed the sack and went over to the scales. A couple minutes later he came back and gave Annie one hundred and eighty six dollars worth of chips, five bingo markers and a tube of glue that she left in the bag. All Annie could say was, "Oops, sorry." Actually that is what they called the weigher: Oops! He got that name because he would drop gold nuggets on the floor. Dropping two or three and picking up one or two, saying, "Oops!"

Loud McCloud said something loud and Annie said, "Shut up, McCloud" which made Good Time Charley a little jealous because he'd never heard Annie tell anyone but him to shut up before. Charley was thinking of going home and strapping on his six shooters. Then he remembered he only had one and that was in the pawnshop. Stopping for a moment, Charley said, "Hey bartender, give me a double." You could hear Annie say from her seat, "Shut up, Charley!" which made him feel a little better.

PART 2

Loud McCloud hollered, "Come on, let's get this game going. Time's a-wasting." Little Annie didn't want to say shut up again but he could see the words in her eyes, so he just leaned back in his chair. A little bit too far and fell over backwards. Boy, when he got back up he was a-cussing, so Tex had to tell him to shut up, which put blood into McCloud's eyes. Things got a little tense and everyone put their hands on their pistols expecting fireworks any minute. Luckily enough, Wyatt Earp came through the door at that moment, and seeing what was happening said, "McCloud you're too loud. Now everyone take your hands off your guns or you'll be playing poker in heaven." Then looking over at McCloud said, "Or purgatory." He didn't want to swear in front of Annie. Everyone knew that Wyatt and Tex were best of friends, so McCloud just grunted and ordered another whiskey. Everyone took their hands from their guns. Tex yelled, "Come on, let's play poker!" Then he said, "Hey, where's that piano player?" Old Fast Fingers as they called him, stuck his head from out behind the piano and said, "Here I am, Boss!"

Veronica was the dealer that night, and with her smile dealt everyone their cards. Tex bet first, Tony raised, Big Al raised, McCloud raised a little higher, and then it became Annie's turn. "Hey Tex," Annie said, "Can I check now?" Tex said, "No, not now. It's sixty-five to you." Annie said, "Just checking. Five, ten, five, five, ten, ten, ten, ten no five, here you go." They all threw their discards in saying, "Give me three," or "Give me two." Big Al said, "Give me a break, I'll take four." Annie said with her best poker face, "I'm good." Tex drew his third ace and he was the first to bet saying, "I'll bet seventy-five." Tony was the first to fold. Big Al did the same. Then McCloud tossed his cards in saying, "I hope you ain't bluffing like you did in Rampart."

Annie said, "All I got is seventy-one and this here ivory bingo marker." Tex said, "Ok, since it's you, Annie." That made Charley a little jealous again. Annie said, "Shut up, Charley!" and Charley said, "Hey, I didn't say anything." Then Annie said, "You don't have to." Anyway, Tex put down his three aces saying, "Here you go, three o'clock. Whatta you got?"

"Nine to five!" Annie said, as she threw down four nines and a five of hearts. "Now that's what I'm talking about," she said under her breath as she reached over the pot, raking the chips in just like a professional card player.

Now them hands were going back and forth all night. McCloud would win and order a whiskey, and when he lost he would order a whiskey, so he pretty much had the bartender running back and forth all night. Annie looked around the room when she noticed that she hadn't heard a sound out of Charley for some time. "Now where's that Charley?" Annie was thinking when she spotted him down at the other end of the bar, good timing. "Nah, don't got to worry."

The pots were getting bigger and the piano was playing more of a slower sound. Loud McCloud completely wore out the bartender. Annie and Tex were still full of energy, Big Al was down to his last cigar, done chewed up at least six. Glue Pot Tony was counting his chips. Veronica shuffled the cards to what was going to become the last hand of the evening. With her smile she dealt the cards out to each player. Tex picked his cards up one at a time, grinning a little wider with each card. Tony took one look at his cards, threw them in and said, "That's it for me. I gotta go open up for the breakfast crowd." Big Al grabbed his cards and started arranging them this way and that way. McCloud snatched his cards up, leaned back in his chair and fell over again. "Hey bartender, whiskey." Annie slowly slid her cards together, bounced them on the table and brought them to her eyes. Four deuces and the queen of hearts. Now, that might be a good hand. But that's not the end of the story.

PART 3

Now the story really begins here. Like everyone knows, Tex and Jack McCloud weren't getting along. Loud McCloud just had to beat Tex at his game and Tex's game was poker, some say the best in the Northwest. Tex was known never to cheat, but he could bluff like no one could. He had the nerves of a polar bear and the coolness of an iceberg. He always had a calculated reason for everything he did or didn't do. He studied his cards, and counting his chips said, "I'll open at five fifteen." Gail said, "I'm out. Gotta hit the trail." Big Al threw his chips in and said, "I'll close at six." McCloud, who by now had a big stack of chips said, "Ok Tex, you opened at five fifteen, Big Al closed at six. That'll make it six fifteen to me. I'm in." Annie said, "Let's see, five fifteen, six fifteen… time out."

"Hey Charley, run down to the Glue Pot and have Tony cook us up some steak and eggs." Then she said, "I'll see your six fifteen and raise five, five, oh, there's a fifty, five." What she was really doing was reading the players. She was thinking, “Big Al lit his cigar... must have a good hand. Loud McCloud was quiet and didn't order a whiskey… must be worried. Tex was too cool… must be bluffing.” Then Annie said, "I’ll raise twenty four seven," as she pushed her chips into the pot. Tex cracked a smile and said, "I’ll see your twenty four seven and raise you another twenty four seven.”

Big Al said, "Too steep for me. I fold." McCloud eye balled his chips, then looked over at Tex. That would only leave him with one chip. "I’ll call and raise you five." He flipped his last five dollar chip into the pot, thinking, “That S.O.B. better not be bluffing!” Annie yelled down to Charley, “Cancel that order!" Then she said, "That's it for me boys. I got just enough to pay J.D. off and get me and Charley a beer.” So with that, Annie threw in her cards and slowly counted her chips. Five, five, twenty five.

Tex said, “I’ll call you McCloud and raise you." McCloud jumped up, threw his cards down and said, "I fold! I hope you ain't bluffing!" Tex slowly laid his cards down one at a time. Ten of diamonds, jack of diamonds, queen of diamonds, king of diamonds. Then he threw the last card face down and said, "You'll never know." Still standing, McCloud put his hand on his gun and said, "You took all my money... draw!"

Tex said, "Now wait a minute, McCloud. The way I see it, I got about three hundred thousand and you ain’t got nothing. So it ain't worth me getting killed. Sit down and order a drink. I’m buying. Matter of fact, I’ll get the house a round. Bartender! Hey wait a minute. Where is everyone?" Then he heard a voice from behind the piano, "Here we is, Boss!" McCloud noticed Tex's body shifted, like he was maybe holding a gun under the table… or was he bluffing? “Whiskey, bartender," McCloud yelled. He wasn't going to take a chance.

Annie said, "Come on Charley, we got enough for a couple of beers down at the Board of Trade." So they said their good nights and walked out the door. Once outside, Charley stopped and said, "Here you go Annie, you can have my split. I never got into the game.” Annie looked into the poke and said, "We're stepping in high cotton now Charley! I told you we were going to make a fortune tonight!" Charley said, "Yep… a small fortune."

"Oh, shut up Charley," you could hear Annie saying as they walked arm in arm down the wooden sidewalk, smiling and nodding to everyone they passed.

It was the end of the night… and the end of this story.

RACE DAY SATURDAY

During the old Gold Rush Days in Nome, Alaska they had a narrow-gauge railroad starting from town, running about 76 miles up into the mountains of the Kougarok Mining District. Many of the miners would use the tracks for a chance to run into town. Or should I say, the dogs would do the running, pulling a contraption they called a Pupmobile. A Pupmobile consisted of a long box with four wheels that would roll on the rails. Some had canvas covers and they looked like miniature covered wagons crossing the tundra. They would harness up their team of dogs to the box and take off. When they reached a decline, the dogs would jump into the box with the driver and away they would go riding down the slope, which was almost all the way to town.

Now the hard part was returning to camp and climbing back up Anvil Mountain. The dogs were always in good shape, but you couldn't say that about most of the miners after a night in town. One time the baker arranged for a race to the top of Anvil and back. He rented the clock that stood in front of Veronica's Jewelry Store and placed it on the starting line facing town. He needed a large one with big numbers so they could watch the time with the Big Telescope from down at the Board of Trade Saloon.

Now the drivers of this Pupmobile race were decided by a drawing down at the BOT, where hundreds of people packed the saloon for a chance to win. It seemed like everyone wanted to race. The baker just needed two drivers. A winner and a loser. So, he held a raffle and sold tickets for a dollar a piece. The first and last ticket out were the winning drivers who would get to race for the $500 gold prize. The first ticket out was The Honey Bucket Man. And the last ticket drawn was Little Annie's. And of course, Annie wouldn't go without Good Time Charley. The baker didn't mind Charley going along. He just figured more weight for the dogs to pull up Anvil Mountain.

Now that Annie won the drawing she had to come up with a plan. The race was a week away and she needed to get herself and Charley in shape. That was the first part of the plan. The rest she figured would come later. One plan at a time. Good Time Charley on the other hand, had his own plan…hide. The first place he thought of was down in the basement of the B.O.T. Then he remembered the little shed in the back that stuck out over the water. No one really knows how it got there, it just showed up one morning after a big storm wedged it between the building and the only rock on the beach. Those big storms rearranged them buildings in Nome all the time. The federal courthouse used to look west, now it looks a little northwest.

Charley overheard Annie telling Denal'ee Rain her plan when Denal'ee was coming off stage after signing "The Blue Forget-Me-Not of Alaska." Charley couldn't hear everything, but he heard Denal'ee saying "Good Luck!" So, Annie must have a hell of a plan. And those plans were the worst because Annie could change them anytime she wanted. Charley figured he could just hide. Not all the time, just some of the time. Just when she had her plan on her mind. Now that was his plan.

"Hey, anybody seen Charley?" Annie yelled over the crowd. "Seed'm going out the back!" someone yelled from the bar. Then another person shouted, "They just made an outhouse out of that old shack back there." Then someone else said, "Yeah, they just cut a hole in the floor. Only open at high tide!" The guy in the corner of the bar shouted out, "Running water!"

"Charley you in here?" Annie said as she opened the door to the shack. No answer. "No Charley, I wonder where he could be?" Annie thought to herself. Then out in the distance she heard a voice sounding like Charley's. "What was that, Charley?" Yep, sure enough, there he was bobbing around on one of them buoys offshore. Annie yelled "'Hey Charley, whatta ya doing out there?" Charley yelled back, "Who in the hell cut that hole in the floor?"

What happened was Charley noticed Annie looking for him in the B.O.T. So he ran to the shack in the back, almost knocking Larry over as he was coming out the door of the shack with a torn-up Sears Catalog. Charley only took two steps inside then down he went through the hole and caught the tide on the way out. "Hang on Charley, I'll go wake up that old Boston Whaler," Annie yelled back. "Hurry up Annie, I gotta gol" Charley shouted.

But first Annie had a plan. She went back inside and walked over to the Big Telescope. She then sighted it right on Charley, and for two bits you could watch him bob back and forth. Best show in town. Well, not the best. Denal'ee Rain's show at the Board of Trade Saloon was the best show around. But Denal'ee paid her two bits and was watching Charley.

So, I guess you can say Charley was the only show in town. Most people paid to look to see if Charley was all right, but after watching a while they just had to laugh and order a beer. Poor Charley was hanging on for dear life and trying to take a nip from that bottle Annie wasn't supposed to know about. "What the hell," Charley thought to himself. "I'm to far out for anyone to see." He didn't think about that Big Telescope being aimed right at him.

Annie put Little Frank the big Eskimo in charge of collecting the money and went to get that Boston Whaler. When she got there, she found out that he went up North on a trip. She had no choice but to go over to the Lifesaving Station and bother those guys. "Hey Annie," Lifesaver First Class Fitzgerald jumped up saying, as she swung open the huge door to the station. "Where's Charley?" Annie said. "Don't ask me how he did it, but he done fell in the Bering Sea and he's out there hanging onto one of them buoys. And he's got that bottle I'm not supposed to know about. On second thought let's leave him out there." Then Annie walked out and swung the huge station door closed.

But Annie had a plan. She knew the Lifesavers would go out and get Charley, but she wanted to set up some betting on how long it would take them to get out there. She had to get back to the B.O. T. fast because them Lifesavers were fast. And before she could take another step, the huge station door flew open and out ran Lifesaver First Class Fitzgerald leading the charge, followed by the rest of the Lifesavers pulling a wagon-mounted lifeboat behind them. Annie got to the B.O.T. before them lifesavers could hit the water.

"Ok, 5 to 1 odds," Annie shouted as she held up a bunch of ones. While they are out getting Charley, it would be a good time to explain the rules of the Pupmobile Race. There weren't any. The baker just came up with the idea of the race. The rules he figured would come along like Annie's plans, one at a time. Besides, sportsmanship in the far North was a thing of honor. There was nothing in the rules about getting an edge. The edge in gambling lingo would be getting a little advantage but not taking advantage. "5 to 1. They're getting closer," you could hear Annie shout, while way out in the distant you could hear Lifesaver First Class Fitzgerald shouting, "Hold on Charley, we're coming." And Charley shouting, "Go back. I like it out here!"

Ding! Annie pulled the rope on the bell, just receiving the signal from Buckaroo Gail, who's turn it was to watch Charley through the Big Telescope. They were laughing so much they had to take turns watching Charley hanging on to that buoy, and by now he had the swinging and a-swaying down pat. When the buoy swung towards town he would hold on tight and when it swung back to sea, he would take a nip or two. Ol' Charley was clever that way. Anyway, the Lifesavers convinced him to come back to shore with them and seeing that he'd taken his last nip, he decided they were right.

The Lifesavers escorted Charley to the B.O.T. and right up to Annie. What a sight he was too, cold, tired and soaking wet with seaweed dangling from his hair. His pals came around patting him on the back, while impersonating him hanging on to that buoy. J.D. the bartender bought all the Lifesavers a drink and poured Charley a cup of hot black coffee, slipping a shot of brandy into it when Annie wasn't looking. Somewhat waterlogged, Charley said, "Annie let's go home." Annie said, "Not yet, I need to tell you the plan."

Charley wanted to get away, but that coffee tasted so good that he hated to leave. "Hey J.D. can I get another one? And if Annie asks, just tell her it's coffee." Annie was settling all the bets taken earlier and when she was done, she made about ten bucks. "Oh well," Annie thought, "Good for a couple hard boiled eggs down at the U.S. Merc." Someone asked Annie how she could remember all those bets. Annie told them she didn't. Everyone knew she would never cheat a living soul, and she knew that no one would try to cheat her if they wanted to keep living. Not really. Annie would always say, "Everyone knows everyone so why cheat your friends?" Big Al came over and said, "5 to 1... five bucks." Annie counted out five bills and thought, "Oh well, we'll just get one egg and split it." Then she thought, "Where's that Charley?" Annie turned around and there was Good Time Charley having a good time. Matter of fact, too good of a time, telling everybody the outhouse story... again. Annie said, "Shut up Charley. Come here. I gotta tell you the plan." Charley said, "No, you come down here. I want'a stay close to this coffee pot."

Day after day went by with Annie planning and Charley hiding. Finally Race Day came. Annie had her plan and Charley was nowhere to be found. Annie looked everywhere. No Charley. "Oh well," she thought, "I'll just do it by myself." Annie had her own Pupmobile. She and Charley built it long ago so Annie could go berry picking out on the tundra. They put a cover on it for rainy days and rainy nights. One rainy night Annie, Charley and all the dogs were in the Pupmobile sleeping when the train came around the bend sounding like a gurgling volcano. The dogs heard it earlier but just thought it was Charley snoring.

"What's that?" Annie said excitedly. "Sounds like a train to me," Charley said. "TRAIN!" they both shouted as they grabbed each other, with the dogs jumping behind them squeezing their heads through Annie and Charley's arms so they could look towards the sound. There wasn't a big bang, it was more like a big bump when the Pupmobile met the train. Not wanting to stop, the engineer just kept on going, pushing that Pupmobile about seventy miles up the line. When there was a dip, the Pupmobile would race ahead then the train would bump them again, again and again all the way to the Jimmy K Gold Mine high up in the Kougarok.

Boy, Annie was mad as she shouted at the engineer, and Charley had to hold ol' Dooley back from biting him. Then the engineer said, "Hey, I'm sorry you guys. I thought you were that Loud McCloud guy." Annie said, "In that case, it's alright. Hey, can we catch a ride back to town with you?" The engineer said, "No problem, just hitch up to the back of the train." Annie thought, "Well, it's gotta to be better than the front." What she didn't know until it was too late was that the train couldn't turn around, so the engineer just put it in reverse and the back of the train became the front of the train. Needless to say, they had the same bumpy ride all the way in. That was the last time that their Pupmobile was on the tracks.

Better get back to the race. Now Race Day brought everyone down to the Board of Trade Saloon. Well actually, half came and the other half went up to the starting line on Chicken Hill about a mile out of town. The ones that stayed behind at the B.O.T. decided it would be easier to watch the race though the Big Telescope. It was kind of funny because they ended up forming a line around the walls. They would take a look through the telescope, then step to the side and go around the bar until it was their turn again. J.D. the bartender just had to stand there and pour them a beer and collect two bits as they passed by. The bar charged 12 and a half cents for a beer and 12 and a half cents for a minute on the telescope. Two bits.

Since the Honey Bucket Man drew the first ticket, he got to start first. He had a topless Pupmobile and his dogs were large, strong and mean looking. And when the gun went off right at 12:00 his dogs took off and started running, pulling the Pupmobile up Anvil Mountain. They looked like they were making pretty good time. When the clock struck 1:00, they were halfway up the Mountain and still going strong. That didn't bother Annie as much as looking for where Charley was. She threw back the cover of the Pupmobile to load two kegs of seal oil and there was Charley curled up sleeping.

"There you are Charley!" yelled Annie. "Been looking all over for you." Charley said, "Been here all morning, didn't want to miss the race. Besides I didn't think you were going to use this old crate." Annie said, "Shut up Charley, and help me tie down these kegs of seal oil and drill a hole behind each of them back wheels. We'll let the oil drip on the track as we go up the mountain. This way those tracks will be nice and slippery when we head back down." You could hear the cannon go off from way out in the distance, signaling that the Honey Bucket Man made it to the top and now was coming back down. "There's the signal," someone shouted down at the B.O.T. "2:15," J.D. the bartender said. Then he added, "I bet it'll take him an hour to cross the finish line."

"You're on! Make it ten bucks," Big Al jumped in saying. "Ok," J.D. said, "but I'm still betting on Annie and Charley to win." Well, it took the Honey Bucket Man about an hour, forty-five minutes to finally make it across the line, crossing just as the big hand struck 4:00. Someone said he rode the brake all the way in. "Ok guys, four hours to beat," Annie said as she and Charley jumped into the Pupmobile right at 5:00. Then off they went over the rails. "Ok Charley, open the seal oil," Annie commanded. Charley gave the knob on each of the kegs a turn and out poured the oil right on the tracks just like Annie had planed.

Making it to the top was a lot of work, but the dogs pulled hard and they made it in just under an hour and twenty minutes. "Hurry Charley, let's get this thing turned around and go back down." The cannon fired as Annie, Charley and the dogs piled back into the Pupmobile. Rolling down the mountain they started picking up speed. Faster and faster they went. "Hey Charley, didn't we put brakes on this thing when we built it?" Annie yelled over her shoulder. Charley yelled back, "Brakes? You said we didn't need any!"

Poor Charley and Annie must have been going 200 mph and picking up speed coming down Anvil Mountain on those oily tracks. The dogs were having fun with the wind blowing in their faces, and Annie and Charley were both holding on as tight as they could. They were getting closer and closer to Chicken Hill. They hit the bottom of Anvil at 300 mph, then they shot up Chicken Hill so fast that they went airborne like a skier coming off a big ski jump. With everybody looking up, they rocketed through the air, flying over the Bering Sea Saloon and landing with a big splash a hundred feet out in the Bering Sea. Charley yelled, "Here comes them Lifesavers." And sure enough there was Lifesaver First Class Fitzgerald leading the charge, running to the water's edge with a life preserver raised over his head and shouting, "Hold on, we'll save you!"

People argued over who won the Pupmobile Race. Some argued that

Annie flew over the finish line, when she should have rolled over the finish line, like the Honey Bucket Man did. But it's not over yet. They still have to hear what Annie has to say about it when she gets back on shore. Which may take some time because Lifesaver No-Class Fitzgerald tripped over a log and got tangled up in the life preserver.

WATCH DUTY

THE DAY WYATT CAME TO TOWN

Good Time Charley and Little Annie were sitting down at the Board of Trade Saloon arguing with each other over who was going to win the big bet they had on the time it takes the first ship to anchor in Nome, Alaska. Now the first ship that year was spotted on Arctic Mary's watch with the use of the Big Telescope they had set up at the Board of Trade Saloon. Everyone in town had to take a turn at "Watch Duty."

"When's your watch?" Annie asked. Charley asked, "Which watch?" Annie said "Dammit Charley, didn't you ask which watch your watch was? I hope you got the morning watch, you'll never make the midnight watch!"

It has to be explained what watch duty was. There was this Big Telescope set up in the back of the B.O.T. looking out the only window in the back and the cleanest window in the joint. That was one of the duties of the watcher. And every watcher took great pride in keeping that window and huge telescope spotless. It was said that they used the best gin in the house to clean the telescope lenses and the window glass. The brass they would shine with plain old spit.

Next to the telescope there was an old card table with only one chair and that was for the watcher to sit and watch. It was the baker who started the betting on the first ship arrival in Nome. Since then, every year everybody would keep an eye and an ear out for the first ship. Then they all would start betting and taking turns watching for the first ship to drop anchor in Nome. The farther the ship was out, the longer the betting and watching lasted. Sometimes it would take a ship a good three or four days to inch its way through the ice. It was quite a sight to see. The Captains used to make grand entrances, blowing their horns and whistles full blast and stoking the boilers to get a good cloud of smoke going.

The betting went sometime like this. You would bet the minute the first anchor hits the water. You had 5 to 1 odds and all you had to do was tell the baker your minute, place your bet and he'd tell you if you won or lost. Before they got the telescope, they would send watchers out by dog team to the edge of the ice. Their job was to send a smoke signal when they spotted a ship.

One time, Little Annie and Good Time Charley spotted a ship on their watch. Annie said, "Hey Charley, start the fire and send out the smoke signal. Tell them a ship is a coming!" Charley said, "How do you make one of them smoke signals?"

"Dammit Charley! I thought you told them you knew how to do that," Annie yelled back. Charley said, "I did?" and Annie said, "Yeah you did! You said that you and Sitting Bull use to sit around together and he 'tot you to read them smoke signals."

"Yeah," Charley said defensively, "I said, I can read them. Didn't say anything about writing them!" Annie thought for a moment then said, "I got me an idea. You start the fire and I'll get that reindeer skin off the sled. Ok, A is one puff of smoke, B is two, 3 puffs is C... I got it. You're going to have to pour some of your whiskey on that fire to get it going!"

"No can do, Annie," Charley said. "Them sled dogs musta got ahold of that bottle. It's empty."

"Yeah right, Charley!" Annie said, not agreeing. "Give me that reindeer hide and let me try it out." Annie took the hide and waved it over the fire, sending up puffs of smoke. Then all of a sudden they heard a loud cracking sound. Charley yelled, "What was that?" and Annie, with a worried look on her face said, "Dammit Charley, you set that fire too close to the edge of the ice and it's breaking off. Hurry, put that fire out."

They started hitting the fire, Annie with her reindeer hide and Charley with his brand new parka. Now as they were beating the fire, puffs of smoke were shooting up. C.W. up at the B.O.T. yelled to J.D. the bartender, "Look, a SMOKE Signal. What does it say?" J.D. said, "It looks like: HELP, CHARLEY'S DRUNK AGAIN."

Not knowing that she was sending signals, Annie sat down and took a break. Charley kept beating the fire while unknowingly sending out signals. "Hey J.D. "What'a that say?" J.D. looked, then turned to Jake and said, "It looks like: SEND MORE BOOOOOOOZE."

Now Charley and Annie were in a bad predicament. They were heading out to sea and the ship was heading into shore. It was early in the evening by then and the dark was not dark enough to see the light of the fire. Not to mention, they were at the edge of the ice, at least five miles out. You could say, "They were," because they ain't there now. They drifted at least another five miles out into the Bering Sea and both of them were totally exhausted from beating the fire out.

"OUT!?" Annie yelled. "Dammit Charley, why didn't you leave some of that fire going!?" Charley said, "Sorry, I got a little carried away towards the end." Then Annie said, "Charley, I hope you got some matches!" And Charley said, "I think them sled dogs took them too. They probably wanted a good cigar with their whiskey!"

"Shut up Charley," Annie said as she was trying to figure out what to do. Then Annie said, "I got it Charley! Remember when that U.S Marshall Tonner came up from Council and got caught on the ice with that dance hall gal? When the ice broke off, the only thing they had to burn was his new dog sled he had custom made in Nome." Charley interrupting her said, "'Yeah, he ended up marrying her." Then he mumbled, "Hey what's this? Oh, whiskey. And what's this? Oh, oh, matches."

"Dammit Charley, I told you to quit smoking them cigars! And another Thing. Can't think of it right now, but there's another Thing!" That made Charley a little worried, because he couldn't think of what the other Thing she meant could mean. But he knew Annie could and would come up with that Thing when he least expected it. "Oh well," Charley thought. "It's always one Thing or another!"

All of a sudden Annie looked up and heading right down on them was this huge ship exhaling thick black smoke. And before they could do anything, there came this deafening screech of the ship's whistle. Charley took a big slug off that bottle and threw it into the small fire that he started while thinking of that Thing. When the whiskey hit the fire, it lit up the sky like the Northern Lights. All the Captain could make out were two people standing there holding each other with a bunch of dogs pushing up around them.

"Ahoy!" the Captain shouted through one of them megaphones, which didn't do any good because the whistle made both of them deaf and the lights almost blinded them. And as far as the dogs were concerned, they didn't know what was happening. They just knew Good Time Charley and Little Annie would protect them like they always did.

Annie heard a voice above her saying, "Hey, which way you heading?" Slowly focusing her eyes, Annie yelled back, "Oh, me and Charley thought we'd go down to China for a couple of days. What'a you think! You some kind of a wise guy? Throw me a rope!" By the sound of her voice, the Captain wasn't too sure of what he was catching from the Bering Sea. Then he remembered catch & release. Besides, it wasn't him that yelled. It was that guy in the long black coat that was doing all the shouting.

With his megaphone pointing up in the air, the Captain called out, "Throw her a rope! Steady as she goes." Annie yelled back, "Don't worry about me being steady, Captain. It's Charley that you gotta worry about." Charley said, "I'm alright." And Annie said, "Shut up Charley." She was still angry at that guy with the big mustache in the long black coat.

"Wait till I get up on deck," Annie told Charley. No one ever made fun of Annie and if they did, she would stop them quick. The First Mate grabbed a rope and heaved it overboard, landing right on top of Annie and Charley and knocking them both off their feet, with the sled dogs yelping as they leaped into the air in all directions. Boy, Annie was boiling mad as she picked herself up off that snow covered chunk of ice that was now bobbing back and forth like Charley walking home from a good night. Looking up, the only person she could see on deck was that guy with the big mustache wearing that long black coat and big black hat.

"Haw, just wait till I get on deck!" Annie was cussing to herself as she grabbed the rope. Charley said, "Ladies first." Annie said, "Shut up Charley! Go get them dogs and I'll climb up and find a basket to load them in." Charley said, "You better find me one too. I ain't climbing up no rope." Then Annie said, "Hey wait. I'll tell them to lower one of them lifeboats and they can just tow us behind them."

With that Annie yelled up to the Captain her instructions. Dutifully the Captain raised his megaphone and shouted, "Lower the lifeboat." Then pointing the megaphone towards Annie and Charley, he shouted, "Ahoy there! Instructions carried out!" Annie turned to Charley and said, "Who's that Ahoy guy anyway?"

"That must be you!" Charley laughingly said. Annie getting madder by the minute yelled, "Shut up Charley. Ahoy my ass! Now go get them dogs together."

"Ahoy Annie!" Charley said dutifully. "Shut up Charley," Annie shot back. It took them all night and half the morning to get close to shore. A huge crowd lined the beach, the biggest turn out ever. Apparently the ship's Captain sent a message to Ft. Davis with one of those flashing lights. Private Anderson reporting to the Colonel said, "A message Sir: AHOY, RESCUED A DOUBLE ON ICE." The Colonel replied, "At ease. That sounds good, I'll have one. Take the fastest team of dogs and tell them guys down at the B.O.T. that they found Annie and Charley. The ship is bringing them in. Now, ON the DOUBLE!"

The trail was rough, but Private Anderson and his dog team were rougher, making the trip in record time. Arriving at the Board of Trade Saloon, he headed right for the bar. Out of breath, he told J.D. the bartender, "A DOUBLE ON ICE." J.D. said, "What kinda whiskey?" Anderson shouted, "No, NO. They found Annie and Charley. The ship's bringing them in now!" And before he could say another word, everyone came around slapping him on the back and thanking him for bringing the message to town.

Now the ship was in sight and what a sight it was. This huge ship was steaming its way to shore towing a lifeboat, Annie standing in the bow with her hair blowing in the wind and Charley sitting in the stern with all the excited dogs wagging their tails in his face and barking. The Captain blew the horn, the crowd cheered, the dogs howled, Annie waved and Charley yelled, "Help!"

"Drop Anchor!" the Captain yelled through the megaphone and the crowd yelled back, "There's No Place Like Nome!" The Captain gave three long blasts on the horn. During the excitement no one seemed to notice the lifeboat floating up close to the ship and not only that, but right under the anchor. Before they knew it there was a big splash, which threw the lifeboat into the air. Annie was still standing but Charley was laying in the back with a pile of dogs on top of him.

The lifeboat shot straight up past the deck, and on the way down Annie came face to face with the mustache guy in that long black coat. Annie wanted to say something but she didn't have time. Then all of a sudden Annie felt a hand grab her arm. Then Annie screamed, "Charley!" as she watched Charley and the dogs falling towards the ice cold water below. Looking up she saw that mustached guy in the long coat leaning overboard holding on to her while she dangled from his arm. Then all of a sudden Annie felt a big tug on her suspenders and there was Charley holding on tight with all the dogs holding on to him. Yeah, what a sight!

It took some doing to get them aboard. No one wanted to let go. The Captain threw over a cargo net and with the help of five big sailors, hauled all of them onto the deck. Turning around, Annie ran right smack into the mustached man wearing the long black coat. "Wyatt, Ma'am," he said.

Annie said, "Why it? What? Why it what?"

"Wyatt Earp!" Charley interrupted saying, "Annie, that's Wyatt Earp, the big lawman from Tombstone down in Arizona or someplace like that." Annie said, "I don't want to know him. Besides, he made fun of me and almost killed us both with that rope!" Wyatt broke in, "Excuse me Ma'am. It was not I who threw the rope. It was the First Mate." Annie said, "I don't care if it was the First Mate or checkmate. You still made fun of me!"

Wyatt took his big black hat off, grabbed Annie's hand and kissed it saying, "Sorry Ma'am" at the same time. Annie never had her hand kissed before and wasn't sure what to say. But Charley did. He said, "Take your hands off that woman and leave your lips to yourself." Annie said, "Shut up Charley, that's what gentlemen do."

"Well, I never done a thing like that," Charley snapped back. While they were out there doing all this talking, the door swung open and out stepped this beautiful woman wearing a long black scarf and a black silk dress. Wyatt said, "I'd like to introduce my wife Josephine." Annie shook her hand and said, "Howdy Ma'am. I'm Annie and this here is Good Time Charley. Nice to meet you." Charley stepped up and bowed, took his hat off with one hand and took Josephine's hand in the other, placing a kiss on that hand. Well actually, he got all those hands mixed up and he kissed his old fur hat. Charley was always good at breaking the ice. Even the dogs were laughing. Matter of fact, it was so funny that it bonded their friendship forever.

Annie said, "Come on Charley, grab them dogs and let's catch the first barge into town. We gotta check in at the B.O.T to let them know the First Ship is in. We're still on duty."

"What duty?" Wyatt asked. "WATCH DUTY!" Annie said as she grabbed Charley by the arm and slowly walked down the deck. Now you would think this is the end of the story, but it ain't. They were still a mile from the beach and Wyatt hadn't landed yet.

To be continued as soon as they find a barge to take them to Nome, Alaska.

HORSE'N AROUND

A lot of people don't realize the importance, or guess you could say the contribution, that the horse made during the Nome Gold Rush. Dog power was great traveling long distances but horsepower was needed for moving mining equipment. Most of the big stuff was hauled by horses in the winter when everything was frozen. Some horses just worked the streets hauling freight up and down.

"Hey Charley, why don't you get a job on one of them wagons?" Annie said as she looked out the window of the Board of Trade Saloon. That was her and Charley's favorite spot to sit there, where they could see everything going on in town. The way they sat, Charley would be looking down the street and Annie would be looking up the street. Not being nosey, just curious. Watching newcomers or spotting old friends coming in from their gold claims.

"Hey Charley. Here comes King!" Annie's favorite horse. "There goes Prince!" Charley's favorite horse. Prince was a huge handsome steed and King was a small white horse. Annie said "I'll lay you 5 to 1 odds that King can beat Prince in a race. "I'll take that bet!" Big Dave the driller shouted. Charley jumped up and shouted, "Prince can outrun that ol' King any day!"

"Oh yeah," Annie said, along with that look that said, "OH YEAH?!"

"OH NO!" Charley whispered into his shot.

"Somebody run and get them guys who owns them horses!" Annie yelled. Then she whispered into her beer. "I'll show that Charley!" The word got out about the big race before there was even a big race... Oh well that's Nome.

Big Steph, the owner of Prince was the first to come through the door. "Hey Annie, I hear you're looking for me. What's up?" he said as he ordered a beer. Annie said. "Charley here thinks your Prince can outrun

King. I got 5 to 1 says he can't."

"Oh yeah, Prince used to race before coming up here," Big Steph said with a not so nice look.

"2 to I," Annie shouted as she held up her hand full of ones. About that time J.D. walked in and said, "Hey Annie, I hear you're looking for me. What's up?" Charley said, "Annie here thinks Prince can outrun your King."

"Shut up Charley. I said King can outrun Prince. Got 5… no… 2 to 1 on it," sneered Annie. J.D. ordered a beer and spoke, "Sounds good. Who's gonna to be the jockey?" Annie said, "What's a jockey?" J.D. said, "Who's going to ride them horses?" Someone way in the back shouted out, "Let Annie and Charley ride!" Charley yelled back, "Who said dat?" Annie said, "I ain't no jockey." Big Steph stepped in and said, "It's Ok with me if it's Ok with you J.D." J.D. said "Yeah, it's Ok with me. Whatta ya think Wyatt?"

"Sounds Ok to me," Wyatt said as he looked at Annie and smiled. "Thanks," Annie said. "No thanks," Charley said. Tex Rickard said, "Charley you ride Prince and I'll knock off the fifty bucks you owe me from that poker game the other night." Annie said, "What poker game?!" then gave Charley that look that says, "I'll see you later." Charley worrying about later said, "Ok, I'm in." Annie said, "Well I'm OUT... Charley gets fifty bucks, and I don't get nothing." Richard the tugboat Captain said, "Hell Annie, I'll give you seventy-five bucks to ride." Annie said, "Make that a hundred bucks and a round for the house."

"You're on," the Captain said as he held up his beer. Then he yelled, "Drinks on Annie!"

"While they're having their drinks, I'll go get the oats," thought Charley. "It's going to be a long night."

They decided to race in the morning before Front Street got too crowded and muddy. Actually, Annie wanted more time for betting. And Charley said he wasn't going to ride on an empty stomach.

Later that night, Annie decided that it was time to go home. "Where's that Charley? He better not be hiding again."

"Hey, Charley?" Annie shouted into the crowd. Someone shouted back, "Seed'm down at the delivery stables eating oats with Prince, and he asked me if I would go get him some carrots for dessert." Back at the barn Charley was talking to Prince about the race and thinking, "Where's that guy with them carrots. Must'a stopped at the B.O.T." The barn door opened and there was Annie. She said, "Come on Charley, let's go home. It's getting late, we got to race in the morning and they won't let you drink and ride."

"Well, that's it for us Prince. See you in the morning," Charley said as he patted him on the neck. Turning around Charley then said, "Hey, where's Annie?!"

"Over here," Annie waved. Annie was talking to King at his stall on the other end of the barn. "Ok King," Annie whispered. "When the gun goes off just start running like them sled dogs do during the All-Alaska Sweepstakes Race. You may be small, but you are faster and smarter than Prince and Charley put together."

"Hey, I heard dat," Charley hissed and Prince snorted. "Maybe not Prince but Charley for sure," Annie whispered loudly to King. That made King let out a horse laugh and Prince couldn't help but laugh too. Then the next thing you know, all the horses in the barn were laughing. "Come on Annie, let's go home. What's for dinner?" Charley said. "Oatmeal," Annie said, making them horses laugh even harder. Charley said, "I'll just wait for dessert. Hey, where's that guy with them carrots?"

Back at the cabin... Annie said, "Hey Charley, what do them jockeys wear?" Charley said, "I'm not sure what you call it. Something pink or green with white riding breeches. Myself, I'm just wearing my old red long-johns."

"Shut up Charley," Annie said as she was looking through some old magazines that came up from Dawson City, Yukon. "Here you go Charley," Annie said giggling. "Here's a horse race at Santa Anna. Hey, I like that name." Charley said, "Yeah, I like that, Santa Annie sounds Christmasie!"

"Shut up Charley," Annie said as she was studying the jockeys. Then she said, "Too bad these pictures are black and white. I'll bet you someday they'll invent a color magazine."

"I'll invent it," said Charley. "Yeah right, like the time you invented that so-called 'snowmobile' with that airplane engine the Professor gave you," Annie said. "Well, it went didn't it?" Charley huffed. "Yeah, it went alright, right through the B.O.T.'s wall!" Annie said as she turned the page.

"Hey, I was thirsty!" said Charley "Anyway, now they got that big window for that Big Telescope you always like to look out of."

"Shut up Charley, I'm always looking for you." Annie said as she turned another page.

This is not the End… just a time out. The End comes later. Besides the Big Race is tomorrow.

ORDER IN THE COURT

LAMB CHOPS VS. HOT DOGS

Many stories unfolded during the great Nome, Alaska Gold Rush and this was one of them.

There was this court case involving this here sled dog and one of the sheep, apparently killing that sheep. Anyhow, someone brought charges against the sled dog, and he was taken into custody. This was going to be the trial of the century, at least for Nome. His lawyer entered a self-defense plea, and the owner of the sheep wanted a murder charge with the death penalty, along with a monetary reimbursement double the amount of what that darn sheep was worth. Now a fine sled dog on the other hand was worth 20 times more than that piece of mutton. Therefore, justice had to be served.

Once the people in Nome found out about the trial, and even though it was the peak of the mining season, their curiosity told them to pack a lunch and spend the afternoon watching one of Nome's top defense lawyers present his case. Now before I go any further, I've got to tell you about the jury selection. Let's see, there was Miss Dunaway who owns the boarding house down by the old Board of Trade Saloon, and Dena'lee Rain who sings down at the BOT, then Old Joe, the swamper at the BOT, and oh yeah, Chillylee, he was the all-around gofer for the BOT. Then there was Good Time Charley and Little Annie, who hung out at the BOT. Once Little Annie came along, they went ahead and swore her in. They were going to have twelve jurors, but since it was the busiest time of the year, they decided to cut it in half. And besides, the other six didn't want to leave the BOT.

"Your Honor, Ladies and Gentlemen of the jury," the prosecutor started. "We d'people accuse this here muddy, scroungy…" and before he could say "flea-bitten dog," the whole court erupted like Mt. Redoubt. That's one thing you never do. You never disrespect a dog, let alone a sled dog, in this country no matter what they might have done. They were ready to tar and feather that poor young prosecutor, who by the way, had just arrived himself and never seen a sled dog before.

Only Little Annie could control the angry crowd. She jumped between the prosecutor and the roaring mob. With her arms spread she stood there keeping everyone at bay. The soldiers from Ft. Davis came in and escorted the prosecutor out, and no sooner than they had him out the door, another big disturbance broke loose. Annie wanted to go with the soldiers and Good Time Charley would not have nothing to do with that and got into it with the soldiers. They were going to arrest him, but Annie said that she was not going to serve if Good Time Charley wasn't going to be there. So, they just let him go.

It was Annie that came to the rescue. She whispered to the Captain that she would see them down at the BOT later. The lunch specials at the restaurants were hot dogs and lamp chops. The ones that wanted the sled dog to win offered hot dogs. And the ones that wanted the sheep to win offered lamb chops.

Anyway, let's get back to the story. You could hear a lot of ruckus and commotion coming from down the hallway. Then in walked this here sled dog looking as though he went 15 rounds with Jack Dempsey, the champion boxer. Besides being muddy, that poor dog I think was still in a daze from the beating he took from that there sheep, which I believe was the first sheep in Nome. And for sure, the first sheep that old Alaskan sled dog had ever seen. There was talk that if convicted, the sled dog should have that sheep for his last meal. Anyhow, the owner of the sheep said that he had the sheep's carcass on ice up at the Nome Icehouse and wanted to know how he should bring it in…frozen or thawed.

Now that there was order in the court, the court was in order. The young prosecutor returned making an apology for his poor use of words describing the defendant. He didn't say it, but he still couldn't see what all the fuss was about. The judge must have noticed this tho, because when the first snow came, he sent that poor prosecutor down the trail to St. Michaels by dog team, to prosecute a con artist who sold tickets for passage on a ship that didn't exist. By the time he returned he knew what everyone meant. When he was crossing the ice, a blizzard blew up and the Bering Sea started to come alive below him. With a total white out and the thin ice heaving, the only thing he could do was tie himself to the sled and let the dogs get him home. But that's another story.

Okay, now back at the courthouse. The trial was to begin again. All the people were settled down and snacking on their lunch. The prosecutor passed the opening statements to the defense. He figured he said too much already. The defense lawyer slowly rolled his chair back. Then he slowly stood up. Slowly he extended his right arm, swinging it slowly towards the defendant laying on the floor. Then he began to speak, slowly. We called him Sloe Gin.

"Ladies and Gentlemen of the jury," he began. "I ask you is this the face, shaggy as it may be?" And before he could say anything else, there came some noise from out the window. It was the loud battering of a flock of sheep being herded from down the street. The noise became louder as they reached the front of the courthouse. The defendant's canine ears popped up and his nose started twitching… he jumped to his feet and started to go through the open window. You never seen Sloe Gin move so quickly, grabbing the defendant saying, "That's ok old boy, don't be scared, I'll protect you!"

Then all of a sudden, Little Annie jumped up and said, "The way I see it, that there ol' sled dog done never seen one of them sheep before. Went over there sniffing around and one of them sheep must have had a bad day. Seeing that they had to travel by barge and swim to shore, then be paraded through town. That sheep probably said, "Enough is enough, I'm going to kill something!" And there with his nose in her butt is this poor sled dog. I say a'quit, because I'm a quitting myself! It's getting late and I have a date. Let's go Charley."

With that the judge threw down his gavel and yelled, "Not Guilty," charging the sheep with aggravated assault, and fining the sheep's owner a round of drinks down at the Board of Trade Saloon for bringing vicious animals to Nome, Alaska. The trial was over and so is this story.

GOOD TIME CHARLEY

GETTING THE GOLD OVER THE TRAIL OR UNDER THE WATER

Annie and Good Time Charley were sitting around thinking how to make some money. All of a sudden Annie jumped up and shouted, "Charley, I got it! Let's enter that there sled dog race! Hey Charley, where did you go?..."

Old Charley slipped out as soon as he heard, "I got it!" because he knew when she got it, he'd get it. He'd had to deal with that "it" before. Like the time Annie "Got it" and took him gold mining on the beach and had him walk out under the surf breathing on a long hose that she was holding up with one hand while steadying herself on a little dingy.

A week earlier, Annie had the blacksmith down at Low's Stables forge an apparatus to her specifications, which she had drawn out on a Board of Trade Saloon bar napkin. It went something like this:

PLAN 1. Connect small fire hose to the top of an upside down milk can. Make sure Charley's head fits into can. Cut a window on side of can so Charley can see out when he's in the can. Use one of Dobb's glass photo plates for window glass. Don't forget to pick up a loaf of bread from Mamie. Fasten milk can to Prince's horse collar. Steal horse collar.

PLAN 2. Find where Good Time Charley's hiding.

Well, Annie found Charley hiding down at the B.O. T. under a big pile of seal skins that "One Shot John" from little Diomede brought in to trade at the Board of Trade. Charley gave him two bits to let him hide under them. He could have gotten away with it if he hadn't been snoring so loud. Annie could recognize his snoring anywhere. She always said he sounded like a walrus in heat.

About fifty people had gathered around the dock watching Annie loading Charley into the dingy. When someone yelled, "I bet that ain't goin' to work!" Annie turned around and yelled, "I'll take that bet. What you give me?" The guy shouted back "5 to 1." Annie snapped back, "I'II take it."

Now you should have seen Good Time Charley standing there not having a good time in his red long johns with that milk can on his head and the horse collar around his neck. He wanted to get it over with but now he had to stand there for another hour while they all made their bets. He couldn't help himself when he shouted out, "I'll bet anyone a pound of gold that it'll work!"

Everyone went silent and Charley thought, "That'll shut them up." Then way in the back of the crowd, New York Neil yelled, "I'll take that bet and I'll even throw in an iPod. Charley looked at Annie and said, "What's An I-Cod?" and Annie said, "Beats me, he's a New Yorker!" Charley yelled, "Ok, But you can keep your I-Cod!"

Annie whispered, "Hey Charley, where are you goin' to get a pound of gold? Charley said "Don't worry Annie, I have full faith in your plan." With a little smile Annie thought, "That's my Charley." Then Annie said, "Ok Charley, give me that bottle." Charley said, "Dammit Annie, it's going to be cold down there."

"I'll send you down some later," Annie said. "Don't worry." Charley thought to himself, "That's my Annie."

The hose was fastened to the bottom of the milk can, supplying air to what is now the top of the milk can on Charley. Not only that, Annie could also hear Charley through the hose. She came across that quite by accident when she rolled out the hose. She was about sixty feet away when she heard a squeaky voice coming from out of the end of that hose. She put it up to her ear and she could hear Charley cussing about her plan. Annie wanted to get mad but couldn't because she was laughing so hard at his squeaky voice coming through the end of the hose. Charley couldn't see what was so funny and started cussing even more as he watched Annie rolling around laughing with that hose in her ear.

Anyway, getting back to the plan and Annie back on her feet. When Annie and Charley pushed off from the dock, New York Neil whispered to Marine Sergeant Pootoogooluk to run down to the Life Saving Station and alert them to the possible life-threatening situation devolving out in the Bering Sea with Annie and Charley. Then New York Neil grabbed the Sergeant and said, "Better not. They might stop him and I'll win the bet. That wouldn't be fair. Just run down there and make sure that old Lieutenant Fitzgerald is on his feet."

The surf was up as Charley and Annie were making their way out of the jetty, when Charley began getting second thoughts about this great plan of Annie's. Charley said to her, “Don't you think we should wait for low tide when the water isn't so rough?” Annie said, “Don't worry Charley, it will be calm on the bottom.”

Then Charley said, "Talking about the bottom, let's have a drink. BOTTOMS UP!" Annie said, "Bottoms up? You better get on the bottom and shut up! Now give me a kiss before you jump."

ALASKA'S FIRST AIRPLANE

A lot of people don't know that the first airplane in Alaska was actually built in Nome, Alaska. Professor Henry Peterson, a music teacher, designed and built the plane in an old warehouse over by the Board of Trade Saloon. The question was, did it fly or not? It all depends on who you ask.

Now take Good Time Charley and Little Annie for an example. They were sitting at the window of the BOT lazily dazing out. All of a sudden they heard the roar of some type of engine, then something rushed by, something huge. Well, needless to say, old Charley looked at Annie, who was looking back at him wide-eyed, trying not to look surprised. She thought it might be better to act like she hadn't seen nothin' and apparently Charley had the same idea, thinking Annie might cut him off and make him go home. But what was that thing?

They didn't need to go out to look because news traveled fast and soon someone would walk in and say something. That was right, because shortly afterwards, the baker walked in looking strange. He wanted to say something but he was afraid the bartender would cut him off before he got started. Annie was the first to speak.

"Did you see or hear anything? Something big, something loud?" Then Charley said, "Something loud, something big?" Annie said, "I just said that Charley," and Charley said, "No you didn't. You said something big, something loud." Then Annie said, "Shut up Charley!" The baker mumbled, "Must of been one of those Alaskan mosquitoes. Hey bartender, ring the bell and get the house a round!"

J.D. the bartender rang the bell and the people from all corners of the bar and a few from outside came in and bellied up to the big spender. They all knew the baker had the dough, and if he didn't they knew he'd go out and make some bread by betting on something, anything! He was a professional gambler. One time he bet on how many times Annie would tell Good Time Charley to Shut Up in an hour. He never said the number. And being Nome, no one really cared. They just wanted to know who won the bet. The bartender didn't want to keep score, so they sent word for the best CPA at XYZ to come down to the BOT, ASAP.

Now the Professor heard the bell from outside and didn't want to pass up a shot and a beer. There he was standing in the doorway covered with mud. Annie waved him over and said, “Hey Professor, you look like you been digging in the mud. Looking for that golden Billiken?" The Professor said, "No, I had to dig my Aeroplane out of Dry Creek, which ain't dry! But am...Hey bartender, I'll take a double on the baker."

Annie jumped up and said, “You had to diga what! An Aeroplane? What in the tarnation is an Aeroplane! You ever hear of one of those things Charley?" Charley nodded and Annie told him to Shut Up again. Anyhow the Professor said, "Its a flying machine." Charley gave him a one-eyed look and said, "A flying what? A flying machine! Think you been flying higher than that plane!" Annie said. "Shut up Charley. Come on, let's go take a gander at that thing."

Crossing the street was no easy task. There were thousands of people trudging through the mud on Front Street and Back Street was even muddier. There were only two streets at the time, Front Street and Back Street. You had the Bering Sea, then Front Street, with two rows of buildings and when you walked out the back of a building on the second row you were on Back Street. Which was kind of confusing, because sometimes you think you're on the second row when in fact you're on the first row, and you go out the back door and end up in the Bering Sea.

When they arrived at the warehouse, the Professor swung open the heavy door and there was this here Magnificent Flying Machine, looking magnificent! When Annie looked at the contraption she thought it was something to help with the laundry. She thought the engine was the washer and the wings for hanging your clothes on and the propeller was to help with the drying.

"When are you going up again Professor?" Annie asked. "I never got up! I need a test pilot. How about you Annie?" Annie said, Yeah sure, but I'm not going unless Charley goes with me.” Charley said, "I'm not going," and Annie said, "Ah shut up Charley, you're going! Hey Professor can you make this thing a two-seater?"

"Yeah," the Professor said. "Grab that old rocking chair over there and some tape on the bench. Matter of fact we can use the tape for your seat belt." Charley interrupted saying "Talking about a belt. Let's go back to the B.O.T for a fast one."

"Oh shut up Charley!" Annie said jokingly.

The Eskimos called the machine 'Tingmayuk' meaning "The Bird" and they called the hill 'Peluk' meaning "No Luck." The plane weighed about 500 pounds, a two-wing job and probably the first ever airplane fitted with four skis. But most of them came to see what Annie was up to, which wasn't easy. The launch pad was at least a mile and a half out of town through the deep mud and snow. Break up came early. And you should have seen Annie. She made a jumpsuit, at least that's what she called it, in case she had to jump she said. Now ol' Charley on the other hand wore his Three Hundred Dollar suit. He figured that if he was going out, he would go out in style. Beside all the Dance Hall girls were going to be on Peluk Hill to see them off.

Anyhow, Annie cut up an old canvas tent for her jumpsuit. She lined it with fur for warmth and padding, and used ivory buttons to hold everything in place. She told someone that she wore three of her best baleen corsets for protection.

The contraption started up. Roaring and shaking with steam shooting and shouting out of every hole like a moonshiner's still ready to explode. ROOM PUTT, PUTT Room!... Then all of a sudden, the Bird started moving and everyone gasped. Annie grabbed the controls and Charley grabbed a hold of Annie as they slid down Peluk Hill picking up speed. Faster and FASTER they went. The plane shot up and started a backflip. Half way over Annie shouted, "Hey, I can see the BOT!" Completing the loop, the plane landed slicker than a whistle on the snow. Now, would you call that flying? Annie sure did!

Charley said, "Are we there yet?" Annie said, "Shut up Charley!" Still partly in shock, Charley said, "Woo, I looked over Jordan and what did I see, but a big old sign saying BOT. I need a drink! I'II see you down there."

Back at the bar, you had people arguing if the plane really flew or not. In came Charley looking confused and without Annie. He sat in his favorite spot next to the window. Annie wanted to go flying again and stayed behind to drag that plane back up Peluk Hill. Now Charley was sitting just kinda looking out the window, counting his blessings and missing Annie while sipping a beer. All of a sudden the damndest thing flew by, looking like that airplane with a bunch of dogs pulling it through the air. And was that Annie waving at him? "Hey Bartender cut me off, I'm going home. Tell Annie I'll meet her there. It's been a long day," Charley said with a surprised look on his face.

What happened was, everyone took off leaving Annie there alone. And by golly she was bound and determined to get that airplane up in the air. Then she came up with an idea. She walked down to the dog lot and picked out 32 of the fastest looking sled dogs. Anyway, she tethered the dogs to the bottom wing with 20-foot lengths of rope. The plan was to have the dogs pull her and use that there propeller to keep the plane off the ground. Everything was going all right until a big gust of wind came off the ice, picking them up 30 feet. Them ol' sled dogs were still running and having a great time. They didn't know what was going on, but they sure were enjoying air-mushing and some say the start of the Iditarod Air Force.

Now did it fly?

Who knows?

PICTURES OF NOME YESTERDAY AND TODAY

NOME ALASKA

NOME

SHEARER & NACHBAR
TI NERS & PLUMBERS

SEPPALA
NORTHLAND

ICE · CO.

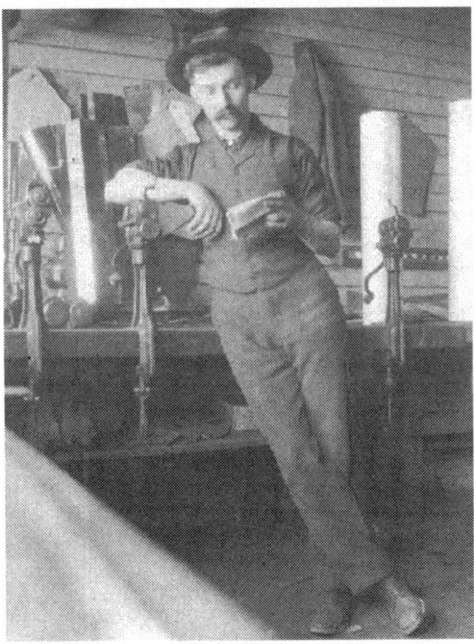

PIONEERS of ALASKA

Made in the USA
Columbia, SC
23 April 2025